SIMON & SCHUSTER BOOKS FOR YOUNG READERS
An imprint of Simon & Schuster Children's Publishing Division
1230 Avenue of the Americas, New York, New York 10020
Text copyright © 2015 by Hot Schwartz Productions
Illustrations copyright © 2015 by Matthew Myers
For information about special discounts for bulk purchases, please contact Simon & Schuster Special Sales
at 1-866-506-1949 or business@simonandschuster.com.
The Simon & Schuster Speakers Bureau can bring authors to your live event. For more information or to book an event,
contact the Simon & Schuster Speakers Bureau at 1-866-248-3049 or visit our website at www.simonspeakers.com.
Book design by Lucy Ruth Cummins
The text for this book is set in Stempel Garamond.
The illustrations for this book are rendered in oil on illustration board.
Manufactured in China
0715 SCP
2 4 6 8 10 9 7 5 3 1
Library of Congress Cataloging-in-Publication Data
Black, Michael Ian.
Cock-a-doodle-doo-bop! / by Michael Ian Black ; illustrated by Matt Myers. — First edition.
pages cm
Summary: "When Mel the rooster gets tired of his boring old cock-a-doodle-doo he decides to shake things up with something brand new—
the cock-a-doodle-doo-bop! But not everyone on the barnyard is a fan of the new tune"— Provided by publisher.
ISBN 978-1-4424-9510-4 (hardcover) — ISBN 978-1-4424-9511-1 (ebook)
[1. Roosters—Fiction. 2. Domestic animals—Fiction. 3. Farm life—Fiction. 4. Humorous stories.]
I. Myers, Matthew, 1960– illustrator. II. Title.
PZ7.B5292Co 2015
[E]—dc23
2014038102

For Eli—M. I. B.   *For Allie, our great entertainer—M. M.*

COCK-A-DOODLE-DOO-BOP!

Told by Michael Ian Black · *Drawn by* Matt Myers

SIMON & SCHUSTER BOOKS FOR YOUNG READERS
New York London Toronto Sydney New Delhi

Hello.

Hey, man.

What happened to "cock-a-doodle-doo"?

Yeah, man. I just wasn't feeling "cock-a-doodle-doo," you dig?

But the sun won't come up without a "cock-a-doodle-doo."

Moo.

Hey, baby, how you feelin'?

To be honest, Mel, I'm a little upset.
What happened to "cock-a-doodle-doo"?

I've been doing that same old number every morning for years. Don't you guys want to hear something new?

No.

I'm concerned the sun won't rise without it.

That's what I said.

How about this . . .

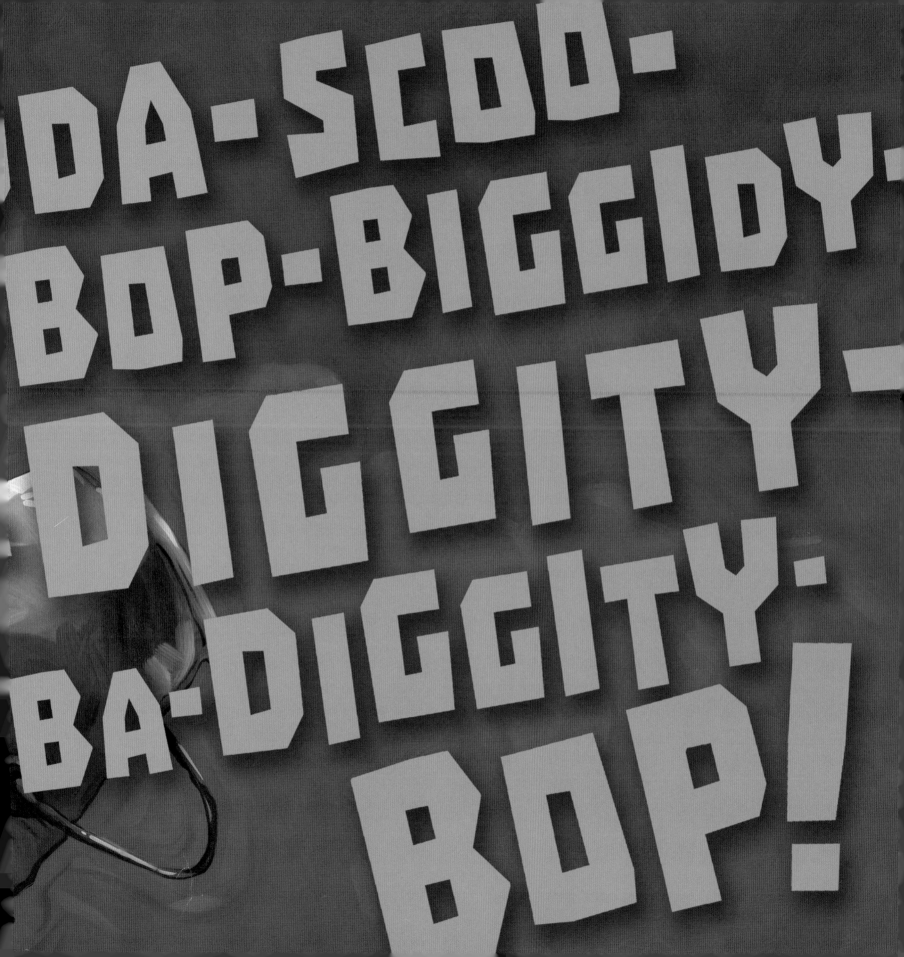

"Cock-a-doodle-doo" is a classic. It's how the sun knows when it's time to wake up.

Without "cock-a-doodle-doo," it might *never* be morning.

Hmmm . . .
Maybe the sun will dig
a little trumpet solo.

Where's the sun?
What happened to
"cock-a-doodle-doo"?
What is going on?

Look, Mel, I'm all for creativity, but some things are perfect just the way they are.

Like eggs
and bacon.

Sorry, everybody, but my heart just isn't with the whole "cock-a-doodle-doo" thing. I got to spread my wings.

Please don't talk about bacon.

Please don't talk about eggs, man.

But without it,
the sun will never wake up!

Hey,
I've got an idea.

Heh—he said "hay."

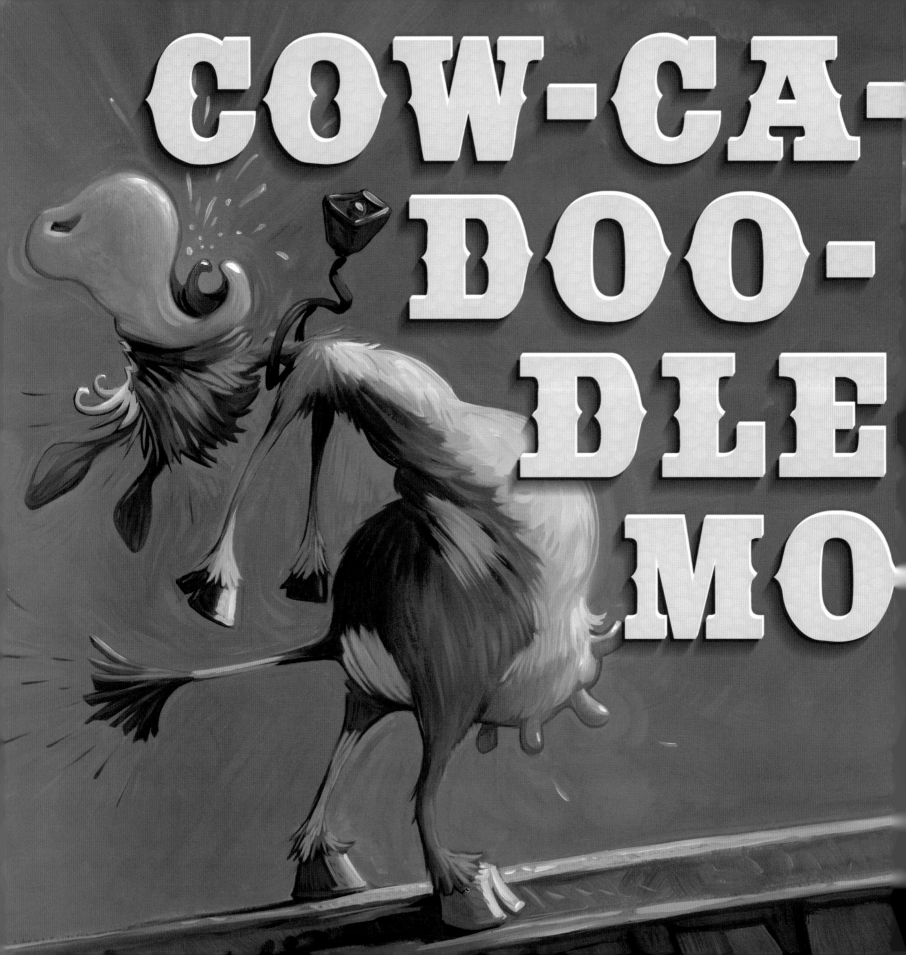

Now we
night owls
can finally
get some
shut-eye.

You said it,
baby.